D0374703

Also in the series:

TEAM TAEKWONDO #1:
ARA'S ROCKY ROAD TO WHITE BELT

TEAM TAEKWONDO #2

BAEOH AND THE BULLY

Master Taekwon Lee & Jeffrey Nodelman

Illustrated by Ethen Beavers

An imprint of Rodale Books
733 Third Avenue
New York, NY 10017
Visit us online at RodaleKids.com

Rodale Kids books may be purchased for business or promotional use or for special sales. For information, please e-mail: RodaleKids@Rodale.com.

Printed in China
Rodale Inc. makes every effort to use acid-free ♾, recycled paper ♻.

Book design by Tom Daly
Additional color by Leo Trinidad

Library of Congress Cataloging-in-Publication Data is on file with the publisher.

ISBN 978–1–62336–947–7 hardcover
IBSN 978–1–62336–945–3 paperback

Distributed to the trade by Macmillan

2 4 6 8 10 9 7 5 3 1 hardcover
2 4 6 8 10 9 7 5 3 1 paperback

CHAPTER 1
Charyeout!
Kyung nae!
Shee jahk!

One! Two! Kick strong! Remember, believe in yourself! Belief is . . .

Belief is . . .

Yes, I can!

You can do it, Ara! I believe in you!
WHOOSH!
ZIP!

Whoaaaa . . . I believe . . . I'm gonna be sick . . .

Yes, you can!

HA!
HA!
HA!
HA!

If you believe in yourself, so will others!
Ahem.

Your kicks are improving, Baeoh, but it looks like you still need to work on your partner skills.

Uhhh, I was just helping Ara come out of his shell faster!
Is it my turn? Where is everybody . . .?

Baeoh, do I need to separate you from Ara again?

No, sir . . .

Sorry, sir. He was just helping me . . .
Yeah, I was helping him with his timing!

Baeoh, I believe it is time you had a new partner.

Yes, sir . . .

Class, please welcome Narsha's buddy, Karhu. Baeoh, he has just begun and will be your new training partner starting tomorrow.
Huh?
성
실

Remember, everyone, that our Buddy Day event is coming up soon. Be a leader like Narsha and make sure to bring a friend. Class dismissed!

Ha-ha! I was watching the trajectory of your kick. It's fantastic . . .
Watching the what?

You know, the way your leg flew through the air. I can't wait until tomorrow. I hope I can duck my head as fast as Ara!

Tomorrow is form day. We won't do kicking drills.
Oh! A form! That sounds exciting! I can't wait!

Must. Eat. FOOD!
Yeah, we're starving. Hurry up!
Me too! I'm coming!
Me thrice. I shall partake in the midday meal.

"Thrice?"
He meant he is joining us for lunch.

I can't wait to fill out a form! Is it a math form or a science form?

If you're watching, Baeoh, it's definitely some form of science.
Yes, and it involves an argument with gravity . . .

HA! HA! HA! HA! HA! HA! HA! HA! HA! HA! HA! HA! HA! HA!

Hey, Baeoh, you okay?

Huh?

Oh yeah. Science! Ha-ha! My form is more like poetry, if you ask me! I am like William Shakespeare.

Poetry! Ha!

Ha-ha! Spear. Ha-ha . . .

I got that.

Oh man, I'm not sure I can eat with you, Baeoh. It's hard to keep my food down!

Hey, Raon! Is that a hot dog sandwich?
YUP! And it is good! What are you eating today?

Yeah, Baeoh! I bet you've got something real good!

Uh . . . yeah. I was so hungry, I already ate my lunch!

Are you always that fast?! I want to be fast, too!
Yup! I guess I'm the fastest cat around! Faster than Ara, for sure!

RUMMMBLE!

Even your stomach tells good jokes!

Hey, Baeoh, I've got an extra hot dog sandwich here with your name on it . . .
Are you sure? Well, if you can't finish it, it's a shame for it to go to waste . . .

BURRRRRRRP!!

Did those guys take your lunch again?
I thought you said you ate it?
What? No, they didn't take it. I gave it to them.

Uhhh, oh yeah! I guess I'm so hungry I forgot that I ate it.
The jackals? Again?
Yeah, they seem to really like my sandwiches.

Baeoh, did the jackals take your lunch again?
Huh? No! Those guys are so funny, and they seem so hungry, I offered it to them.
Then why did you say you ate it?

Are those jackals picking on you again? Are you being bullied?

Honestly, those guys are just playing around.

Thanks for the sandwich, Raon! It was great! Later.
Hey! Wait up.

CHAPTER 2

Maybe this time, they won't be waiting for me in the canyon again.

Wait, last time I wasn't ready. This time, I just need to be ready for it!

Let's do this! Hiiiiii yaaaaa!

Aaaaah! My foot!!!

Okay, tree . . . You caught me off guard. You won't get away with it again. Because this time . . . I'm coming from the air!

Hiiiiii-Yaaaaaa!!

That tree is so tough!

Don't worry, Baeoh, I'll help you up!

Auuhgghrr?!?!?!
Are you okay?
I'm fine. You should see what the other guy looks like.

Thanks for the help.

I mean, I don't need help.

I was just practicing my form and lost my balance. I'll see you tomorrow.

On the morrow!!! That's Shakespeare! I can't wait to practice my form with you!

Oh, Mr. G, you can't go just yet. We're not done with you . . .
Come on, Daegu, let me go. Dubu? George?

Okay, George, if I pass that line, I will hold a record of 100 wins to your zero! Are you ready?

ZING!

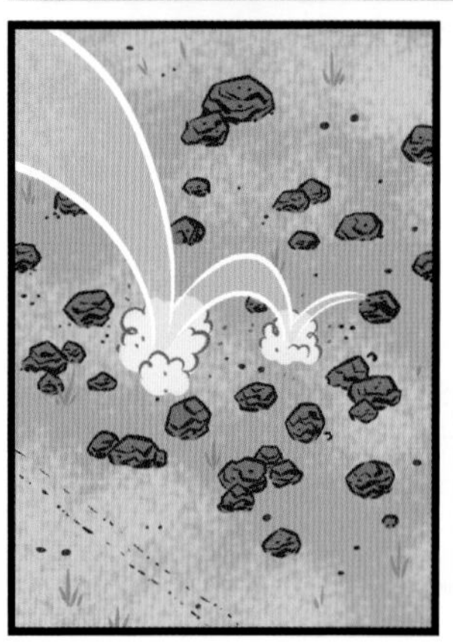

Yes! I win again! I am the champion!!!
You are the best! You always win. I've got to practice some more.

There goes Dubu again. And poor George, I can't tell which one is the rock.

Oh Mr. G . . . here's your chance to shine.

Dubu! George! Fetch my pet back!

Stop that mouse!!

Go, little dude. Run!
Thanks!!!

Why did you do that? You're gonna get in trouble.
Why do you pick on him? He's so much smaller than you.
And I'm smaller than Daegu . . .

That. . . .
. . . mouse
. . . is so . . . . . .

Faaast.
SPLAT!

You two have failed me again!

And you . . . Looks like you owe me a new pet.

Let's see what I can take instead . . .

I'll take that,
thank you.

Give me
that stick!
SWIPE!

Now for
the finishing
touch . . .

Give it back or . . .
Or what?

Never mind.
Thanks, Baeoh. Such a nice gift while you find my pet and bring it back to me! And don't forget extra ketchup on my hot dog tomorrow! Ha-ha!
Yeah, extra ketchup! Ha-ha!

Baeoh, thanks for helping me out. Those guys are so mean.

Yeah, glad I could help . . .

CHAPTER 3

Charyeout! Kyung nae!
성

Baeoh, where is your belt and your gear?

Umm, my friend borrowed them and forgot to give them back. He's pretty forgetful! He'd forget his head if it wasn't attached to his body!

HA-HA! Hopefully he doesn't forget his body, too! Don't worry, Baeoh. I remember everything! I'm a good buddy!

Baeoh, if friends are training without good guidance, then you are giving them blind leadership.

Blind leadership? But I can see just fine. Ara, can you see what I am saying?

I see exactly what you're saying! Don't worry, Baeoh, I'll remind your friends. Just "bear" with me until we see them again!

Uh . . . okay. Thanks.

Baeoh, you need to bring your friends in to train with us during Buddy Day.
Class, switch partners!

Besides, who needs sparring gear when sparring a snake?

How'd you . . . ?
You didn't think I could kick?

Uh, I just wasn't ready for that. I'll be ready next time.

Here, maybe you should wear this.

No thanks. I got this! I just need to keep an eye on that tail of yours! It's out of control!

WHACK!

Didn't see that one coming . . .

Ahhh, much better . . .

How did you fly with no arms? How did you kick with no feet? How did you fly up and kick me so fast . . . with no arms or feet?

Twice?!

You should have belief in others. Just because I don't have any arms or feet doesn't mean I don't believe in myself.

How did you learn to believe in yourself so much?

My parents, my friends, and Master Jahngsoo teach me to have belief.

When you think you can't, sometimes all you need to do is say . . . "Yes, I can!"
That's easy for you to say! You can . . .

Hey, Baeoh, you wanna walk home together?
Yeah, that's a great idea! Let's hurry. Can't be late for dinner again!

Remember, fitness test next week!
Wait a second! Gotta practice for the fit test!

Hmmm, practice for the fitness test . . . or eat a hot dog sandwich?

Eat a hot dog sandwich? . . . Yes, I can!!!!

Catch up to you in a bit, Baeoh!

CHAPTER 4

Narsha is one tough snake! Who knew?

Oh man, even your jokes are getting pretty empty!

Even on an empty stomach, I can still tell a good joke!

YES, I CAN! HIIII YAAAA!!!

Oh boy . . .

C'mon, Raon, where are you?
Can't be late for dinner again. Belief is . . . "Yes . . . I . . . can . . ."

Welcome back, pussycat! We've been waiting for you!
Where's my pet mouse?

Your mouse? Uhh . . . he's a little . . .

. . . trapped at the moment!

Trapped? How'd he get trapped?
Yeah, how?

In a mousetrap. But you should really be asking, "Who cut the cheese?"

He cut the CHEESE!!!

So, guys, how's your training going?

Huh? What training?
Ha-ha!

SMACK!

You should come to Buddy Day and train with me!

CRACK!

You're not my buddy! Ha-ha! Can you see what I am saying?

Yes . . . I . . . can . . .

. . . can WHAT?

I thought so.

Don't forget my pet mouse. See you at your Buddy Day!
Yeah, we'll introduce your black eye to a buddy.

CHAPTER 5

JUNGLE
What happened to your eye?
Whoa, that's shiny!
Nothing.

You ARE being bullied by those jackals.
. . .

What? Bullied? My friend Bruce can help us!

Come on, guys, I don't need any help.

You need to tell the teacher.

7x7 =
Billy

It's not a big deal. I've already invited them to Buddy Day.

Buddy Day! That's a great idea! I'm bringing Bruce. Maybe we can all be buddies!

Bruce is not my friend. He's not my buddy. I don't even know him. I don't even know why I am talking to you?!?

I don't need anybody's help.

What's up with Baeoh?

He's getting bullied. I think he needs help.

Maybe you can show him how to stand up for himself.
. . . ? . . .

Come on, Karhu, let me show you a couple of things . . .

Charyeout!
Kyung nae!
Shee jahk!
Rotate your body for more power!

Find your trajectory to kick with accuracy!
There's that word "trajectory" again . . .
Make good eye contact or lose precision!
HUH?
Ouch!
Precisely. Beware. Lack of focus will make your other eye sore.

You need more practice for your Buddy Day demo.
Narsha can help you prepare for your challenges.
Challenges?
I have more than one?

And why would Narsha help me?

A true leader must have belief in the society around him. Narsha is a strong leader. She shares this belief.

Besides, how else will you show the jackals that you are stronger than them?
Wait, jackals? How does he know?

Did you tell Master Jahngsoo?
No.
Hmm, it must have been Cheeri!
Nope, Cheeri isn't here yet.

Ooooh, I get it. That little bear sure has a big mouth!

Thanks for telling the entire world, Karhu!
Huh? What are you talking about?

Everybody knows you lost your headgear. I brought you one, so you can borrow it.

I told you I don't . . .
. . .

. . . deserve such nice treatment!

You're gonna need it more than me . . .

Better put on that helmet!

성실

Uh, do you have another helmet I can borrow?

Huh?

Have a seat.

Why do you treat Karhu like that?

He bugs me. He seems smarter than me, and that really bugs me!

So you don't like smart people?

That's not what I said! I said, "He bugs me!"

I think you should think before you talk . . .

I think you don't know what I'm talking about.
I don't think you know what you are talking about either.

I do think you are ready for your lesson now. Stand up!

Oh no . . . not again . . .

There is no chance you're going to take it easy on me? It's been a hard day so far . . .

WHACK!
WHIP!
THUD!!

What happened to that kicking bag?

I was training . . .

Yeah! Right! You can't do that. You don't have any hands or feet! You just CAN'T!

When will you learn. . . .

I didn't know you could do that!

I never let anybody tell me what I can't do.

Somebody said that you can't destroy a kicking bag . . . ?

실
Kicking bags?

What's bothering you? You're not your usual self.

Usually, I like eating hot dog sandwiches while wearing my sparring helmet, but then I can't hear my own thoughts because the chewing noises get too loud, so I gave my helmet away . . .

Speak honestly.

The jackals are bullying me, and I don't know what to do.

Why don't you just stand up to them?

Well, there are always three of them on the way home. I'm just outnumbered.

성실
Three is more than one, but remember your friends are here to help you. You need to trust your friends.

Having belief in others is a very important part of being happy.

I just wish those jackals would treat me the way they want to be treated.

Oh, so you like being bullied?

Me? No, why do you say that?

I figured if you treat others the way you want to be treated, then it's very clear that you want to be bullied.

성

HUH? Who in their right mind wants to be bullied?

Never mind.

Wait a minute ...treat others the way you want to be treated. If I like being bullied ...then who am I bullying?

I don't even know who I'm talking to!

Wait up!!

You've got me all confused.

I DON'T like being bullied! It's terrible!

I know the feeling.

You get bullied, too?

I did all the time, but not anymore.

Why would anybody bully you? You're tougher than nails!

Oh, Baeoh, you have such a short memory.
When I was younger, I went to school at the Lizard Academy.

Ss Tt Uu Vv Ww Xx Yy Zz
MATH
Billy
1+1=
Every time it was my turn to solve a math problem on the blackboard, all of my classmates would make fun of me. I had to learn to write with my tail.

I had a hard time making friends, too.
Join the CHESS CLUB
DANCE!
NOTICE
They wouldn't be your friend because you wrote with your tail?
No, because they thought that all snakes were mean.

When I played baseball, nobody thought that I could catch . . .

Nobody even thought I could do Taekwondo.

Hey! Don't worry, I learned my lesson!

Wow! You are so strong. I am amazed at your strength and belief in yourself!

It takes a lot of practice, but anybody can do it. Actually, after a while, it's pretty easy.

Easy? I don't think so.

Yes, I can!
HUH?
You just have to start by saying this over and over.

Yes . . . I . . . can???
NO.
Oh, okay, sorry.

You might as well just give up.
Yeah, you're right. Tomorrow is Buddy Day, and the jackals are gonna show up and make a fool out of me. I should just quit.

You feel better now?
Uh yeah. Now that you mention it, I do! Thanks!

You're welcome!

Okay.

Okay . . .?

You told me to stop, and I believed you.
HUH?

Belief starts with yourself. You have to believe in everything that you do. If you have belief in yourself, others will believe in you, too.

But I don't always have belief in myself.

That's okay. You can practice with confidence.

First, you need to have strong eye contact!
Strong eye contact.

Then, you must stand tall, with your chest out, chin up!
Stand tall!

Then, you must speak with a confident voice.
LEAVE ME ALONE!
Leave me alone.
Louder . . .

Leave me alone!!
If you want me to believe you, make me believe you!

LEAVE ME ALONE
ROAR!

Narsha?

Well, that's a side of you I haven't seen . . . or heard before.

Now that's what I call a confident voice!
Thanks, Narsha!

What is going on out here? Everyone okay?

Yes, sir! We're good.

I was just practicing belief in myself!

Very good, Baeoh. When you believe in yourself, others will believe in you, too!

Believe me! I know!
HA! HA! HA! HA!

Narsha, it looks like young Baeoh has passed the first test. Did he pass the second test?

I'm not so sure, sir.

Hey, guys.

I just heard a big roar. Everyone okay?

Yes, Karhu. We are all doing good. What would you do, anyway? Thanks for asking, but you can go home now.

Sorry, Baeoh. I just heard a big noise and wanted to make sure everyone was okay.

Thank you, Karhu, that is very responsible of you.

Thank you, sir.

I gotta run!
Remember, Baeoh, treat others the way you want to be treated . . .

Strong eye contact.
Stand strong. Loud voice.

Belief is . . .
"Yes, I can!"

Huh? I guess it's working already! If I believe in myself, I can do anything!

Hey, Buddy!

See you tomorrow! Can't wait to give your black eye a new buddy!

CHAPTER
6
WELCOME BUDDIES!!
START

They snuck up on me yesterday. Now I'm ready. A strong voice is a confident voice.

Remember to make strong eye contact.

I gotta stand strong.

Hello!

Hey, everyone, meet my buddy!

Get back . . . Leave me alone . . . Gotta keep strong eye contact . . .

Hey, Buddy!
AHHRRGG

Leave me alone!

정 실

What's Karhu's problem?

Karhu was just standing up for himself.

How do you like it when others treat you without respect?

Wait, you don't think I have been doing that to Karhu? I'm the bully?

I think you owe Karhu something.

Karhu?

What?

I want to apologize for being mean to you.

I didn't even realize this whole time that I have been treating you the same way that the jackals are treating me. That isn't right.

Well, I'm sorry.

That's okay! Apology accepted! Let's put the past behind us and be buddies!

Really? Gosh, I've been thinking about the jackals so much, I guess I didn't even realize that I was bullying you.

Don't worry about those guys! My good ole buddy Bruce is gonna be here! He'll help us out!

Karhu, I'm sure your little friend Bruce is nice and all . . .
But I think we got this . . .
Yes, I can!
Look at this place!

성
Team Tigers, line up for demo team action!
YES, I CAN!
Begin demo team action!

And now for the grand finale! Baeoh's board break!

This is gonna be easier than I thought!!

See you outside. Your buddy's waiting!!!

성실

Don't worry, Baeoh, it was a good demo.

We know you can break those boards. You just need to put your weight into it.

Maybe it's because of all those missed lunches. You'll get it next time, after you eat a little something.

Thanks . . . I think.

I'm not worried about the boards. Those jackals are waiting outside for me.

Wait up for us . . .

Okay, Baeoh, let's go.

Hey, pussycat! You need your friends to help you break your boards?

Don't worry, Baeoh, we can help.

Thanks, Karhu, but I have to take care of this myself.

I got a new buddy here just for you!

I don't want to fight.
Fight? Who said I want to fight? I'm just here to introduce you to your new buddy!
Leave me alone!
I don't want to fight!
I'm warning you!

LEAVE ME ALONE!!
Fighting is not right.
Treat others the way you wish to be treated. Your choice . . .

Belief is "YES, I CAN!"

Thanks, guys, for having my back.

I've got a feeling those guys won't be messing with you anymore.

But if they do, we'll be right there with you!

Thanks, guys. There is strength in numbers.

Is it supposed to rain?
Nope, that's just my buddy, Bruce.
Oh, right . . .
That makes sense.
Here you go. I think this is yours.
Thanks. You want to stick around for a while?
THE END!

I PROMISE:

TO BE A GOOD PERSON,
WITH KNOWLEDGE IN MY MIND,
HONESTY IN MY HEART,
STRENGTH IN MY BODY,
TO MAKE GOOD FRIENDS,
AND...
I WILL BECOME
A BLACK BELT LEADER!

TEAM TAEKWONDO BELT RANKS

BARON

NARSHA

MIR

CHOA

SURI

RAON

CHEERI

BAEOH

ARA

ARA (A-RA)

Ara is a shy turtle. Before joining Team Taekwondo, he usually just stayed in his shell. Now he is making new friends and loves to do his forms nice and slow.

Name means: "of the sea"

Belt rank: white

Favorite move: knife hand strike

BAEOH (BAY-OH)

Baeoh is the funniest tiger ever. He has a big heart and loves to laugh. He is everyone's friend but sometimes lacks confidence.

Name means: "flying tiger"

Belt rank: orange

Favorite move: side kick

CHEERI (CHEER-Y)

Cheeri is the hardest worker in the class. Even though she always makes straight A's, she is always trying hard to get better, maybe sometimes too hard.

Name means: "to defend"

Belt rank: yellow

Favorite move: round kick

RAON (RAY-ON)

Raon is the biggest member of Team Taekwondo. He is very strong and a great athlete. Although he always means well, sometimes he leaps before he looks.

Name means: "lion"

Belt rank: camo

Favorite move: reverse punch

SURI (SUR-Y)

Suri comes from a big family of bald eagles. He is small for his age and sometimes tries to act bigger than he really is. He always goes too fast but is working on slowing down.

Name means: "eagle"

Belt rank: green

Favorite move: jump front kick

CHOA (CHO-AH)

Choa is a rare phoenix. She is very pretty and likes it when the other animals do things for her. She is learning to do things for herself, and when she does, she is awesome.

Name means: "light of the world"

Belt rank: purple

Favorite move: double knife hand block

MIR (MEER)

Mir is a super smart dragon. He might not be the most coordinated, but he tries really hard. He is learning to control his strength.

Name means: "dragon"

Belt rank: blue

Favorite move: hook kick

NARSHA (NAR-SHA)

Narsha is the nicest cobra you'd ever want to meet. Even though she doesn't have any arms or legs, she is one of the best in her Taekwondo class. She always works hard but keeps a smile on her face.

Name means: "flying high"

Belt rank: brown

Favorite move: tail strike

BARON (BAR-ROON)

Baron is the highest rank in his Taekwondo class. He is a great leader; he just doesn't know it yet. He is always willing to help.

Name means: "righteous"

Belt rank: red

Favorite move: palm strike

MASTER TAEKWON LEE is a sixth-degree black belt and master instructor with many years of experience with ATA International—the world's largest martial arts licensing company. He's also the creator of the award-winning interactive children's video series Agent G. He lives in Little Rock, Arkansas.

JEFFREY NODELMAN is a graphic artist, novelist, painter, and award-winning animator who has worked with Walt Disney, Warner Bros., and Nickelodeon. He is a fourth-degree black belt trained in ATA Songahm Taekwondo and a USA-certified ice hockey coach. He lives in Little Rock, Arkansas, with one wife, two children, and three spoiled rescue dogs.

ETHEN BEAVERS is the illustrator of comics for DC Comics, Dark Horse Comics, and IDW Publishing, as well as numerous kids' titles, including the *New York Times* bestselling series NERDS. He lives in central California. Visit ethenbeavers.com.

THANK YOU FOR READING TEAM TAEKWONDO.

WE HOPE YOU ENJOYED IT!